We're not making mountains out of molehills.
We're making world wonders.

Write to Keep On (Keeping On): 300-Plus Writing Story Prompts for a Coming-of-Age, Love Story, and More Drama
Copyright (c) 2023 Hakeela Buford / AF.FORD MEDIA, LLC

For information:
AF.FORD MEDIA, LLC
15774 S La Grange Road, Ste. 265
Orland Park, IL 60462
www.affordmedia.co

BOOKS
An Imprint Division of AF.FORD MEDIA, LLC

Printed in the United States of America

ISBN 979-8-9852114-8-1 (print) ISBN 979-8-9852114-9-8 (ebook)

Book Design By AF.FORD MEDIA, LLC
Courteous credits to Robbie Down on Unsplash and Janko Ferlič on Unsplash for respective front and back cover photographs

Robbie Down
Instagram - @robbiedownmusic
robbiedownmusic.com

Write to Keep On (Keeping On)

300+ Writing Story Prompts for a Coming-of-Age, Love Story, and More Drama

Hakeela Buford

To all of the diamonds, rocks, ropes,...and mountains

who are constant reminders of our own strength

INTRODUCTION
INTRO

What this book is not is a route.
It's a pair of shoes to navigate to the route you will
choose.

What it isn't is a trope
(although we all like a good one
every now and then).
It's an audience awaiting your victory.

It's purely just a side companion
for your journey.

And if the world is also just a stage,
you're about to make it
the most legendary one yet.
So, let's open the curtains
and your creative mind
and its unique brand of tenacious ingenuity
to pull out your imagination and

keep us crying and feeling —
but only to carry on.

THE CLIMB
Trapped in four walls

Take the meanest person you've ever known, the sweetest person you've ever known, and the most neutral person you've ever known. Put them in one room. Give them one tough circumstance.

THE CONQUER
What happens?

THE CLIMB

"If that's how you felt, why didn't you just say that?! Instead of saying it like THIS?!!!"

THE CONQUER

What happened? Who is this character speaking to? What did the other person do?

THE CLIMB

A pack of Oreos
A horse racing track
An '80s model muscle car
A ranchhand
A judgment of dissolution

THE CONQUER

THE CLIMB

A cigarette bud
An eviction notice
An arcade
An Orlando Magic fan

THE CONQUER

THE CLIMB

"No excuses! You were supposed to do it and didn't. Now, I have no other choice but to…"

THE CONQUER

What next? Who is the character speaking to? What is the consequence?

THE CLIMB

A player's shot goes in on the court inside of a stadium, and in the audience, a girlfriend smiles apologetically at her boyfriend. He hangs his head, and she leaves.

THE CONQUER

Why? What next?

THE CLIMB

A clock on a city billboard counts down to the new year. As it expires and the fireworks begin, your character gets down on one knee in front of their partner. And the partner...

THE CONQUER

THE CLIMB

"You know? I'm ready.
...I think I'm finally ready."

THE CONQUER

Finally ready for what??

THE CLIMB

What starts off as a good summer instantly turns into tragedy over night.

THE CONQUER

THE CLIMB

A person is running desperately down a street then suddenly stops and sighs outward, "It's too late."

THE CONQUER

Too late for what? And is it really?

THE CLIMB

An old journal
A courtroom
A kid who has an infection
A bill collector

THE CONQUER

THE CLIMB

A couple break out into laughter together. Then it quiets down. And then they both go mute, looking at the other. And then they cry.

THE CONQUER

Why?

THE CLIMB

A parent wakes up their child in their bedroom with a homemade birthday cake, but the child doesn't smile. Instead, the child ask, "Isn't this weird? Since...you know...what just happened?"

THE CONQUER

What happened? And what can be done (if anything) to make this moment lighter?

THE CLIMB

A pack of Twizzlers
A train
A teen who gets suspended
A case of food poisoning

THE CONQUER

THE CLIMB

"I tried to unsee it in you. But it's obvious that you're..."

THE CONQUER

Who is this character speaking to? How can the person on the receiving end make the character see differently (if at all)?

THE CLIMB

"I tried to forget. But I just can't. Especially when…"

THE CONQUER

"Especially when" what?
What happened? What can
be done to ease the character's
mental state?

THE CLIMB

"Yeah, when he stepped in, he immediately shook his head in confusion because the doctors said he might not recognize anything for a while."

THE CONQUER

What happened to the
character being discussed?
How will he heal?

THE CLIMB

A shell of one's self…with bones to pick

A cowrie shell
A human skeleton model
A college lecture hall
A professor living in the past that's filled with many skeletons

THE CONQUER

THE CLIMB

"I keep calling. Even though I know it's pointless, I keep listening to that ring. I have to."

THE CONQUER

What is the emotional connection to the phone calls? How can this character get better?

THE CLIMB

A pair of siblings have to navigate their own path to safety when a _______ comes through their neighborhood while their parents are gone.

THE CONQUER

THE CLIMB

A jazz club
An electric car
A meat factory
A traveling artist

THE CONQUER

THE CLIMB

"I could've said so many things. And instead, I said…"

THE CONQUER

What did the person say? Is it something that has destroyed a situation? Bond? Opportunity? How will they fix it?

THE CLIMB

"I don't think I can stand to hear that voice again, man."

THE CONQUER

What is the emotional here? Whose voice can't the character handle? How can this character get better?

THE CLIMB

"One more night. Just tough it out one more night."

THE CONQUER

What is the significance of this final night?

THE CLIMB

"This here will be our downfall, boys."

"Nah...We've already fallen."

THE CONQUER

...Or have they? What is the context here? How do they see victory in whatever that means for them (and you and your story)?

THE CLIMB
Wonder and Wander

"Sometimes, I wonder _______.
Then other times, I wander _______."

THE CONQUER

THE CLIMB

"I can't make her love me...But I'm damn sure going to try my hardest to persuade her."
"Did you forget the part where she's a prosecutor?"
"When I first met her, she was a DA. Until I persuaded her."

THE CONQUER

THE CLIMB
All about the smiths

A Granny Smith apple
A granny with the last name Smith
The Smithsonian
A locksmith in deep trouble

THE CONQUER

THE CLIMB

Practice makes perfect. But one collegiate coach might be taking it a bit too far. At least, according to the athletes' parents...and the one star athlete in charge of it all.

THE CONQUER

How does the coach respond? What happens next?

THE CLIMB

A secret
A promise
A promise broken
An ultimatum

THE CONQUER

THE CLIMB
Cuttin' up

A box cutter that is instead used for...
A die cutter who falls for...
A haircutter with a secret...
A woodcutter workshop where...

THE CONQUER

THE CLIMB

A group of young friends persuading one of the newest members to commit a seemingly harmless act leaves not just the new one but all of them with drastic consequences. Even the friends who tried to flee the scene.

THE CONQUER

THE CLIMB

A couple's date to mend some mutual resentments doesn't go as planned.

THE CONQUER

THE CLIMB
I Love the '80s

A Ghostbusters film poster
A glow in the dark Pineapple Ind ghost figure
A Cabbage Patch Kid
An Atari
An answering machine

THE CONQUER

Challenge: Incorporate all of these vintage items into your story...But not actually set in the 1980s. What are your characters tackling?

THE CLIMB
I Love the '70s

A Salem's Lot film poster
A park
A pair of corduroy bellbottoms
A box of Hamburger Helper
A war vet

THE CONQUER

Challenge: What is the story here? And no, it can't be actually set in the 1970s.

THE CLIMB
I Love the '90s

A Yo-Yo
A Sony Discman
A Bart Simpson T-shirt
A plaid or color-block shirt
A New Jack City film poster

THE CONQUER

Challenge: All of these vintage items lead to your character's ruin in some way.

THE CLIMB
Workin' with whatcha got

A house without any furnishings
A fridge without any food
A car without an engine
A skateboard without any wheels
A middle-aged person without any kids or spouse

THE CONQUER

Incorporate all of these
elements into your story.

THE CLIMB
Without one's better half

A pajama bottom but no top
A sock without its pair
An earbud missing its other
A manila folder void of its long-gone documents
A person who just got dumped

THE CONQUER

Incorporate all of these
elements into your story.

THE CLIMB
It's not over.

A leftover meal
A layover in an airport — for the second time
A hangover
A voiceover heard on the way to something
A turnover

THE CONQUER

Your story's just begun.

THE CLIMB

A kid
A new stepfather
A bag of Chinese takeout
A pair of loafers
A beach house

THE CONQUER

THE CLIMB

A stormchaser
A deodorant irritation
A dermatology office
A stolen credit card

THE CONQUER

THE CLIMB

A health club
An electric toothbrush
A typewriter
An employee thinking of job hopping

THE CONQUER

THE CLIMB

A stolen identity
A rental application
A leaking faucet
A school
A new divorcee

THE CONQUER

THE CLIMB

A landlord nursing a troubling habit
A credit report
A verdict
A stack of sheet music

THE CONQUER

THE CLIMB

A civil engineer
A stolen blueprint
A bus station
A tablet

THE CONQUER

THE CLIMB

A kid with a disability but who won't give up
A sweatshirt with a hole that just won't be thrown away
A frozen TV dinner
A church with a recurring leak

THE CONQUER

THE CLIMB
Say cheese

A smiling family portrait
A cheesy word of advice
A cheesy song
A cheesy meal
A cheese platter at an event that turns bad

THE CONQUER

THE CLIMB

A disparaging comment
An employee benefits office
A holiday weekend
A retiring sociologist

THE CONQUER

THE CLIMB

"If you don't tell him soon, she will…"

THE CONQUER

What is happening here? What is this piece of important news that "she" will share? How will it affect everyone?

THE CLIMB

A heart monitor
A pack of rubber bands
An underground operation
A single parent

THE CONQUER

THE CLIMB

"A gamble on you would be a gamble on my ____. Why would I play like that?"

THE CONQUER

What is the source of conflict here? Who is vocalizing this conflict, and why don't they trust the other?

THE CLIMB

"A match went out last night. And I ain't talkin' one in a ring."

THE CONQUER

What has lost its flame or spark?

THE CLIMB

A vegetable stir fry
A magic trick
A stack of dusty vinyl
An auto shop
An increasingly impatient customer

THE CONQUER

THE CLIMB

"How can you honestly be laughing right now after what you did?"

THE CONQUER

What happened? How can the shamed person be absolved by the speaker, if at all?

THE CLIMB

A rainy day
A phonebook
An abandoned shopping cart
An herbalist

THE CONQUER

THE CLIMB

A rusty car
A tub of ice cream
A convention center
A last will and testament

THE CONQUER

THE CLIMB

"There are some people who are just
unforgivable. You're one of them."

THE CONQUER

What happened? How can the shamed person be
absolved by the speaker, if at all?

THE CLIMB

"You have an interesting logic. You don't want me to _____, but it's perfectly reasonable for you to _____."

THE CONQUER

What is this speaker accusing another of? Why are they upset? Is it justifiable? How can the accused fix this?

THE CLIMB

A kennel
A new appliance
A public meltdown
A missing piece of jewelry

THE CONQUER

THE CLIMB

"I only have five bucks. You think they'll give us one more chance?"

THE CONQUER

THE CLIMB

"You can't ____, but you can screw up my life. That's rich."

THE CONQUER

What is this speaker accusing another of? Why are they upset? Is it justifiable? How can the accused fix this?

THE CLIMB

"Can you tell her I said hi? Oh, and that she's still full of crap?"

THE CONQUER

Although this line is funny, the circumstances around it tell a different story. What's that backstory? How does it end?

THE CLIMB

"Give me a reason why I should care anymore?"

THE CONQUER

Challenge: This can't be a comment surrounding a romantic relationship.

THE CLIMB

"Sometimes I wonder what it would've been like if that had never happened.

...Ya know?"

THE CONQUER

No, we don't know. So, fill us in. What is the story here, and how will the speaker go on?

THE CLIMB

"I don't like eggs, and I finally admitted that. What's taking that a step further and saying the same about you?"

THE CONQUER

Although this line is funny, the circumstances around it tell a different story. What's that backstory? How does it end?

THE CLIMB

"My life. Look at it. How'd I get here?"

THE CONQUER

"Coming this far gives me no choice but to keep seeing how much farther this gas tank of mine will push me."

THE CONQUER

What has your character been through? How is that fueling them now? Is it? Will they make it to their goal?

THE CLIMB

"Did you ever stop to think that maybe they, too, are _______?"

THE CONQUER

What is the story here? How is the speaker calling out the other character's self-centered way of thinking?

THE CLIMB

"I like to keep it simple. Life has shown me it's better that way."

THE CONQUER

THE CLIMB

In these following lines spoken to or by your character, draw the next steps to a (hopefully) more positive ending.

"Call somebody who cares.

This line? It's out of service."

THE CONQUER

THE CLIMB

"I say all of that. And all you can say is THIS?!!"

THE CONQUER

THE CLIMB

"It's a weird thing. Sometimes, I cry when I think about.

Then other times, I _______."

THE CONQUER

THE CLIMB

"I'm gonna put it all out there. All of my all. And if it works, awesome…And if it doesn't, _____."

THE CONQUER

THE CLIMB

"I didn't want to.

But I saw no other way."

THE CONQUER

THE CLIMB

"The soap operas called. They want their antics back."

THE CONQUER

THE CLIMB

A womanizer
A victimizer
A tranquilizer
A stylizer

THE CONQUER

THE CLIMB

A soup kitchen
A mail carrier
A heist
A manila envelope

THE CONQUER

THE CLIMB

A movie theater
A gold bracelet
A sous chef
A blackmail attempt

THE CONQUER

THE CLIMB

Things from the past
still have a place in the present.

A fax machine
A typewriter
A newspaper editor
A rotary phone

THE CONQUER

More specifically, they're in
your character's present.
Tell the story.

THE CLIMB

A video clip
A magazine clipper
A hair clipper
A transcriptionist of forensic clips

THE CONQUER

Talk about the transcriptionist's
dangerous position they land in.
And how they (hopefully) get
out of it.

THE CLIMB

A coupon code
A cheat code
A barcode
A coding instructor

THE CONQUER

THE CLIMB

A recluse
A new vehicle
A spoiled piece of meat
A remote work meeting space
A misunderstanding

THE CONQUER

THE CLIMB

A broken rib
A milkshake
A spa
A towed car

THE CONQUER

THE CLIMB

"Yeah, I'll own that; smoking's bad for you.

But so is ______."

THE CONQUER

THE CLIMB

A person with attachment disorder
A new co-worker
A paintbrush
A tire shop

THE CONQUER

THE CLIMB

A recipe book
An AOL email account
A manicure
A music streaming curator

THE CONQUER

THE CLIMB

"A lemon is a lemon.

And sweetening it up won't change that."

THE CONQUER

THE CLIMB

A career counselor
A chocolate chip cookie
A civil lawsuit
A mechanical pencil

THE CONQUER

THE CLIMB

A pair of yoga pants
A coroner's office
A down-and-out artist
A crowded sidewalk

THE CONQUER

THE CLIMB

A (lackluster) report card
A library card
A Black Card
A failed credit check

THE CONQUER

THE CLIMB

A money order
A stuffed animal
A police report
A bank

THE CONQUER

THE CLIMB

A champagne bottle
An award speech that goes bad
A long criminal record
A person with epilepsy

THE CONQUER

THE CLIMB

A rice cooker
A Motown memorabilia piece
A personal assistant
A fish named Andre

THE CONQUER

THE CLIMB

A work-study student
A loan
A warehouse
A grassroots organization

THE CONQUER

THE CLIMB

A swimming pool floatie
A detective
A foyer
A photograph

THE CONQUER

THE CLIMB

A mail order
An infomercial
A kitchen
A twin who's dropped out of school

THE CONQUER

THE CLIMB

A leased car
A bundle of broccoli
A laboratory
A clothes hanger

THE CONQUER

THE CLIMB

A farm
A desktop computer
A sweatband
A bridal shower

THE CONQUER

THE CLIMB

A comedy show
An engagement ring
A leaked text message thread
A violinist

THE CONQUER

THE CLIMB

A bachelor party
A person recently acquitted
A panic attack
A lakefront

THE CONQUER

THE CLIMB

A New Year's party
A software engineer
A rumor
A forest preserve

THE CONQUER

THE CLIMB

A birthday party
A person who has just divorced
A bad case of stutters
A theme park

THE CONQUER

THE CLIMB

A bachelorette party
A person fresh out of physical therapy
An argument
A patio

THE CONQUER

THE CLIMB

A graduation party
A person obsessed with sunflower seeds
An inappropriate joke
A hallway

THE CONQUER

THE CLIMB

A Christmas party
A person who keeps on forgetting _____
A news report
A basement

THE CONQUER

Baby Fever
The following stories incorporate babies, but they all go in starkly different directions.

THE CLIMB

A baby gender reveal party
A person with a fear of bodily fluids
A life-changing verdict
A farmers' market

THE CONQUER

THE CLIMB

A baby shower
A person suffering from imposter syndrome
A depressing monologue over mistakes
A tunnel

THE CONQUER

THE CLIMB

A baby's first steps
A person full of apathy
An assigned project that must be passed
A culinary arts school

THE CONQUER

THE CLIMB

A pregnancy announcement
A person with a growing email inbox
A diagnosis of MS
A rehab center

THE CONQUER

THE CLIMB

A baby's first birthday party
A person obsessed with Picasso paintings
A sarcastic apology
A playground

THE CONQUER

THE CLIMB

A baby's baptismal
A person with relentless headaches
A long, tense car ride
A passive aggressive sequence of replies

THE CONQUER

THE CLIMB

The first word you think of beginning with A
The first word you think of beginning with B
The first word you think of beginning with C

THE CONQUER

The first word you think of beginning with D has to do with the conflict.
Then use all of these words to make your story.

THE CLIMB

The first word you think of beginning with A
The first word you think of beginning with B
The first word you think of beginning with C

THE CONQUER

The first word you think of beginning with D has to do with the location.
Then use all of these words to make your story.

THE CLIMB

The first word you think of beginning with A
The first word you think of beginning with B
The first word you think of beginning with C

THE CONQUER

The first word you think of starting with D is the pivotal action your character does. Then use all of the words to make your story.

THE CLIMB

The first A-word you think of: The place
The first B-word you think of: The main person
The first C-word you think of: The problem

THE CONQUER

The first D-word you think of:
The climax
Put all of the words together
for the story.

THE CLIMB

The first A-word you think of: Antagonist details
The first B-word you think of: Backstory details
The first C-word you think of: Counterplot deets

THE CONQUER

The first D-word you think of:
Dialogue that ignites it all
Put all of the words together for
the story.

THE CLIMB

The first A-word you think of: A fear
The first B-word you think of: An enemy's action
The first C-word you think of: A call to action

THE CONQUER

The first D-word you think of: An item that sparks everything
Put all of the words together for the story.

THE CLIMB

The first word you think of beginning with pre-
The first word you think of beginning with re-
The first word you think of beginning with non-

THE CONQUER

Then use all of these words
to make your story.

THE CLIMB

The first word you think of ending with -ion
The first word you think of beginning with -lap
The first word you think of ending with -ful

THE CONQUER

Then use all of these words
to make your story.

THE CLIMB

The first word you think of ending with -meter
The first word you think of ending with -izer
The first word you think of ending with -tion

THE CONQUER

Then use all of these words
to make your story.

THE CLIMB

The first word you think of ending with -end
The first word you think of ending with -ed
The first word you think of ending with -dog

THE CONQUER

Then use all of these words
to make your story.

THE CLIMB

The first word you think of ending with -side
The first word you think of ending with -est
The first word you think of beginning with -con

THE CONQUER

Then use all of these words
to make your story.

THE CLIMB

The first word you think of ending with -ing
The first word you think of ending with -er
The first word you think of ending with -show

THE CONQUER

Then use all of these words
to make your story.

THE CLIMB

The first word you think of containing 'ess'
The first word you think of containing 'tox'
The first word you think of containing 'plain'

THE CONQUER

Then use all of these words
to make your story.

THE CLIMB

The first word you think of containing 'main'
The first word you think of containing 'plain'
The first word you think of containing 'dain'

THE CONQUER

Then use all of these words
to make your story.

THE CLIMB

The first word you think of containing 'can'
The first word you think of containing 'mid'
The first word you think of containing 'tone'

THE CONQUER

Then use all of these words
to make your story.

THE CLIMB

The first word you think of containing 'sake'
The first word you think of containing 'make'
The first word you think of containing 'lake'

THE CONQUER

Then use all of these words
to make your story.

THE CLIMB

The first word you think of containing 'cane'
The first word you think of containing 'lane'
The first word you think of containing 'pane'

THE CONQUER

Then use all of these words
to make your story.

THE CLIMB

The first word you think of containing 'pen'
The first word you think of containing 'net'
The first word you think of containing 'mat'

THE CONQUER

Then use all of these words
to make your story.

In these lines spoken to or by your character, Fill In The Blanks to a (hopefully) more positive ending.

"Get in the ____. Then get out the ____. You mess up either of those steps, you're _______."

"I said, '______.' You, in turn, said, '______.' And then, everyone else said that we were ______."

"You've got it all wrong. I wasn't ______. I was ______. But you're not trying to hear that."

"To my right, I've got ______. To my left, there's _____. So, looks like I'm at a dead end."

THE CONQUER

THE CLIMB

"I don't care about _____! What I care about is ______! Why can't you and everybody else understand that?!"

THE CONQUER

THE CLIMB

"I feel _____, but I think _____.

...And I'm confused about which to listen to."

THE CONQUER

THE CLIMB

A self-help book
A travel booking to Paris
A bookstore
A bookkeeper

THE CONQUER

THE CLIMB

A shopping cart
A kid trying to master cartwheels
A cartload of mail never delivered
A cartopper that serves as a piece of evidence

THE CONQUER

THE CLIMB

A Super Bowl announcer
An old sinkbowl
A bowling alley
A bowl of ice cream

THE CONQUER

THE CLIMB

A bottle of antifreeze
A rattling sound
A front lawn
A person with a speech impediment

THE CONQUER

THE CLIMB

A lighthouse
A struggling moonlighter
A porchlight that keeps being broken
A happenstance during twilight

THE CONQUER

THE CLIMB

A dogmatic podcaster
A sheepdog
A dogfight in an old film
A dog's incessant barking

THE CONQUER

THE CLIMB

A cabin
A cabin in a truck
A cabinetmaker
A cabinet that reveals something

THE CONQUER

THE CLIMB

A backyard full of leaves
A person who grows shinleafs
A neighborhood leaflet that's central to the story

THE CONQUER

THE CLIMB

A music instrumental
A concert
A luthier who repairs string instruments
An instrument with a certain significance

THE CONQUER

THE CLIMB

A pot that definitely needs to be thrown out
A pottery class
A potter with a bad habit

THE CONQUER

THE CLIMB

A damaged cassette tape
A growing teen with a case of tapeworms
A bad storm that slowly tapers off

THE CONQUER

THE CLIMB

A Cracker Jack bag
A growing crack in a home
An actor most known for a Nutcracker play

THE CONQUER

THE CLIMB

A mailhandler who is considering sending a piece of mail themselves to a certain someone about...

THE CONQUER

THE CLIMB

A student's failed test, which ironically proves to them that they aren't a failure but rather a success

THE CONQUER

THE CLIMB

An awkward but much-needed conversation between an off-duty therapist and their...

THE CONQUER

THE CLIMB

A last dance between a dancer and their...

THE CONQUER

THE CLIMB

A last song between a singer and their impending ex...

THE CONQUER

THE CLIMB

A long, silent car ride between two people en route to...

THE CONQUER

THE CLIMB

A person whose fate depends on getting an approval for a particular loan

THE CONQUER

THE CLIMB

A couple's anniversary date that ends with a relationship-ending confession

THE CONQUER

THE CLIMB

A car mechanic who must pay for a mishap on a customer's vehicle…and not talking money

THE CONQUER

THE CLIMB

A person whose innocent everyday routine lands them in the wrong place at the wrong time...and the right place at the right time for the criminal who plants something on them there

THE CONQUER

THE CLIMB

A writer goes to extreme depths then reaches their downfall for the perfect story

THE CONQUER

THE CLIMB

A person whose plan to execute a birthday surprise goes more and more wrong to an unimaginable end

THE CONQUER

THE CLIMB

Two business partners who don't want to talk about that **one** thing. But they both know they must...

THE CONQUER

THE CLIMB

A photo in a family album that unlocks a painful memory

THE CONQUER

THE CLIMB

Just drive.

A rideshare driver who gets pulled into a crime

THE CONQUER

THE CLIMB

A cake decorator whose livelihood depends on winning a newly televised competition series

THE CONQUER

THE CLIMB

An aspiring college student with a learning disability who plans to defy all odds

THE CONQUER

THE CLIMB

A social worker whose latest client has a dilemma they can't help but to get more invested in than they should

THE CONQUER

THE CLIMB

'Twas the night before Christmas.
And what happens that night might make
Christmas obsolete...

THE CONQUER

THE CLIMB

A person gets excited when they find a long-lost item they've been looking for. Then they get angry. Because...

THE CONQUER

THE CLIMB

In the moment of giving thanks at the dinner table during Thanksgiving, one of the family members gives a shocking revelation...

THE CONQUER

THE CLIMB

There would be no Christmas if there was no Easter.
...An Easter family gathering and its tragic end proves that it won't be a merry next few days. Or months.

THE CONQUER

THE CLIMB

A phone upgrade
A relentless wheeze
A freight operator
A track field

THE CONQUER

THE CLIMB

An ex-convict's New Year's resolution will be harder to achieve than ever imagined when...

THE CONQUER

THE CLIMB

Madison, Wisconsin
An unmarked vehicle
A cartoon character-themed balloon
A tax auditor

THE CONQUER

THE CLIMB

A late food delivery...with the wrong order
A box of tissue
A risky stock portfolio
An email strategist

THE CONQUER

THE CLIMB

An argument about raisin bread — but of course, it's not really about raisin bread

THE CONQUER

THE CLIMB

An English professor having an uncomfortable personal conversation with another but through the use of euphemisms to express their thoughts...

THE CONQUER

THE CLIMB

A late event plan
A flower bouquet
A pizzeria
A lawyer steadily losing clients due to...

THE CONQUER

THE CLIMB
Taking out the trash

What starts off as a quick run to the store for trash bags turns into a trigger, psychologically transporting a person to the past they've been trying to trash from their memory...

THE CONQUER

THE CLIMB

A ski mask
An upcoming deadline
A late employee
A principal's office

THE CONQUER

THE CLIMB

A license plate reader
A subpoena
A hotel lobby
An esthetician

THE CONQUER

THE CLIMB

An old car engine
A poor credit report
A reformed person
A town hall

THE CONQUER

THE CLIMB

A stale coffee
A decision that needs to be made
An uninspired author suffering writer's block
A helicopter

THE CONQUER

THE CLIMB

A struggling politician
A second trimester pregnancy update
A kitchen pantry
A pair of old running shoes

THE CONQUER

THE CLIMB

A highlighter pen
A missing person
A lounge
A malfunctioning GPS

THE CONQUER

THE CLIMB

A missed phone call
A diamond ring
A funeral home owner
A church backroom

THE CONQUER

THE CLIMB

A disappearing pet
A delay in worker's compensation
A summer home
A sleeping mask

THE CONQUER

THE CLIMB

An emergency procedure
A penmanship book
A daycare staff member
A Jamaican resort

THE CONQUER

THE CLIMB

A mop
A tax discreprancy
A nanny
A training facility

THE CONQUER

THE CLIMB

A fracture
A caregiver
An immediate dissolve of a business deal
A truck filling station

THE CONQUER

THE CLIMB

A coloring book
A pending payment
An upcoming Division 1 college athlete
A townhouse community

THE CONQUER

A histogram that reveals something major
A public diss
An injured athlete
A corporate office

THE CONQUER

A ticket on a car
A roadside diner
A data analyst
An auditorium

THE CONQUER

A loner
A lesson plan
A plain sweater
A press conference

THE CONQUER

THE CLIMB

A personality clash
A fur coat
A methodical business professional
A locker room

THE CONQUER

THE CLIMB

A recent lottery winner
A mysterious symptom
A legal proceeding transcript
A laundry room

THE CONQUER

THE CLIMB

A flip phone
A person always putting the cart before the horse
A plaid cardigan
An airplane

THE CONQUER

THE CLIMB

A bowl of piccadillo
A mountain biker
A limo ride

THE CONQUER

THE CLIMB

A mail return
A first week on a new job
A food cart

THE CONQUER

THE CLIMB

A news reporter
A conspiracy
A box of candles

THE CONQUER

THE CLIMB

A ligament injury
A stubborn duel
A red carpet

THE CONQUER

THE CLIMB

An awkward award acceptance speech
A zipline park
A poor relationship with a teammate

THE CONQUER

THE CLIMB

A determined shoe designer
A water cooler
A conversation around that water cooler that
really turns into...

THE CONQUER

THE CLIMB

"You know what? You're a character! You *really* think you're believable after you…"

THE CONQUER

What did the other character do? How can they redeem themselves?

THE CLIMB

"I wanted to go there at first. Thought it was the place to be…I finally get there. And honestly, it was forgettable because…"

THE CONQUER

THE CLIMB

"You're a doctor. And you make me SICK! Ha, figure that one out."

THE CONQUER

How did these two characters get here? How can they get back to a good place?

THE CLIMB

"It's not so much what was said but what wasn't said. Including…"

THE CONQUER

THE CLIMB

"If you don't do it for him, at least do it for me."

THE CONQUER

What is the speaker asking for here? Who are they speaking to? What happens next?

THE CLIMB

"Sometimes, I see a lot in this place. Then other times, I think I should've just listened to Dad…"

THE CONQUER

What is being discussed here? What does this speaker regret? How, and can, it be resolved?

THE CLIMB

"This whole thing's been like eating chocolate after a long time. You've wanted it so bad, but after a few minutes, it can be too much.
But the difference here is I can't just throw this away..."

THE CONQUER

THE CLIMB

"I have to self-sabotage. I just have to. In some kind of twisted way...
...it gives me a thrill."

THE CONQUER

Can this person turn over a new leaf? How?

THE CLIMB

"Well, it's happening tonight whether we like it or not. So, the real conversation we need to be having right now is...how will we react? How will we move forward?...
Will we?"

THE CONQUER Yeah.
Will they?

THE CLIMB

"I'm giving it two days at best. Then, he'll be singing a different tune. He always does. And this time, when he does, I'm singing a different tune, too. I'm going to..."

THE CONQUER

Who is this speaker talking about? What will the speaker be doing? Why? What will happen next?

THE CLIMB

"All I'm saying is this: They have one more time to _______, and then, I'm going to _______."

THE CONQUER

Who is "they?" What have they done? And what does it mean for future events?

THE CLIMB

"Don't you know I was almost five minutes away when she called and told me...?"

THE CONQUER

What conflict has happened here? Who is "she?" What happens next?

THE CLIMB

Buy Now, Pay Later financing
A periodic table of elements
A disrupted vacation
A new attorney

THE CONQUER

THE CLIMB

A bad accent impersonation
A bathtub that needs refinishing
A one-person date to a concert
A person who struggles to articulate their...

THE CONQUER

THE CLIMB

A reverse mortgage
An almanac
A person who keeps yawning
A sinkhole that occurs in...

THE CONQUER

THE CLIMB

An old jar of gel
A dropped restaurant reservation
A person sitting alone at a table
An overheard conversation

THE CONQUER

THE CLIMB

A person with a major concern
A new bill in political office that fuels the concern
A rooftop
A coupon booklet

THE CONQUER

THE CLIMB

A ticket to a play
A long roll of paper
A person dealing with general anxiety
A crowded living room...and not because of a festivity

THE CONQUER

THE CLIMB

A sparkling water beverage
A person who is scared to age
A stood-up date
A hard yoga pose

THE CONQUER

THE CLIMB

A mediator
A cup of tea
A vintage Chevy van
A person who is finally willing to have a
conversation about...

THE CONQUER

THE CLIMB

A beach towel
Two people exchanging bizarre texts
A rejection (Challenge: Not romantic)
A long internal dialogue

THE CONQUER

THE CLIMB

A cold call
A disappointing party
A garden
A person with has nothing but a...

THE CONQUER

THE CLIMB

A controversial pact
A torn page
A cottage
A person who wants to live off the grid...but can't admit to a larger want...

THE CONQUER

THE CLIMB

An unrequited crush
A live podcast tour
A financial aid office
A person who used to play in a band

THE CONQUER

THE CLIMB

A missed three-pointer
A person debutting in...
A hockey stick
A dated slang term

THE CONQUER

THE CLIMB

A harmonica
An unspoken promise
A VIP section
A person who needs to...

THE CONQUER

THE CLIMB

A person trying to get an item on a top shelf
A leopard print piece of clothing
A foreign language
A viewing room

THE CONQUER

THE CLIMB

A person with a shopping addiction
A foundational issue in a home
A forged check
A shoe department

THE CONQUER

THE CLIMB

A city growing with crime
A public statement
A car's backseat
A person who wants to...

THE CONQUER

THE CLIMB

A person with a child they put up for adoption
An email
A surgery that has been put off
A grammar school gymnasium

THE CONQUER

THE CLIMB

A conversation where every other sentence is hard to make out
...
But what's said at the end is very clear...

THE CONQUER

THE CLIMB

A conversation starts on a sports game and ends on a tax discrepancy

THE CONQUER

THE CLIMB

A conversation that starts as a joke and ends with a grave punchline...
Ends with a statement that really hurts because one person tells another that...

THE CONQUER

THE CLIMB

An argument in a store aisle leads to a purchase of juice...
But here's the unforunate reason behind the purchase...

THE CONQUER

THE CLIMB

A conversation winds around forever until finally getting to the main point about...

THE CONQUER

THE CLIMB

A person runs into someone from high school...an old crush.

THE CONQUER

THE CLIMB

An argument between characters that includes:
A chipped tooth
A mounted TV
An injured bird outside a front door

THE CONQUER

THE CLIMB

A reason for a divorce that includes:
A barbecue
A note
A bottle of body spray

THE CONQUER

THE CLIMB

A disappointing interview that includes:
A rattling AC
A sudden ringtone
A protest outside

THE CONQUER

THE CLIMB

A misinterpreted text conversation that includes:
A forgotten grocery list item
A compliment that wasn't taken well
A statement ending with an exclamation point

THE CONQUER

THE CLIMB

An excuse for a late arrival that includes:
A parking lot space
A pack of soda
An omelet

THE CONQUER

THE CLIMB

A tense parent-teacher conference that includes:
A piece of gum
A class assignment
A nervous habit exhibited by...

THE CONQUER

THE CLIMB

"When the going gets tough, I get going.

And it's about time I change that."

THE CONQUER

"Starting by..."

THE CLIMB

"I never understood that. Them...
Being unable to eat or sleep just because someone wants to leave you.
...But now, I know. And I know it's..."

THE CONQUER

What is the backstory of the speaker's heartbreak? How will they heal? Will they?

THE CLIMB

"What I'm about to say will piss you off, but it has to be done...
You are..."

THE CONQUER

How can the accused person prove otherwise?

THE CLIMB

"So, at one point am I supposed to care?

Especially when you're still working on arriving at your own sense of care?"

THE CONQUER

Why does this speaker feel like the other doesn't care? What can be done? Can anything be done at all?

THE CLIMB

"When did she come back?

And when were you going to tell me??"

THE CONQUER

Why is the speaker unenthused about "her" return? Who is "she?" What has "she" done in te past? What can be done now?

THE CLIMB

"What goes up, must come down.
…
Guess I learned my lesson, huh?"

THE CONQUER

What has the speaker done to wind up in this downfall? Can they rise again? How will they?

THE CLIMB

"I can't say I'm surprised. But I will say that I'm disappointed."

THE CONQUER

Why is the speaker disappointed?
How can this matter change?

THE CLIMB

"I'm gonna bet that you didn't even..."

THE CONQUER

Why is the speaker addressing?
Why do they doubt that person,
and how can it be repaired?

THE CLIMB

"Give me three years, and I'll be..."

THE CONQUER

Where will the speaker be? How? Why is it
important? Why will it take three years?

"I haven't seen her smile like that since…"

Who is "her?" and what's her story? What is the speaker's story? Why is this smile so important?

"There is a difference between promising and doing. When will you understand that?"

Why is the speaker addressing? Why do they doubt that person, and how can it be repaired?

"I can't go back there, man. I just can't."

Where is "there?" Why can't the speaker go back? Or can they, and they just have to be brave enough?

THE CLIMB

A box of brown rice
A car suddenly cutting off another
A song that abruptly stops

THE CONQUER

THE CLIMB

A mailed check
A day of constant visits
A person who claps their hands very hard

THE CONQUER

THE CLIMB

A box of cereal
A trumpet
An ambulance

THE CONQUER

THE CLIMB

A video game cartridge
A bottle of cologne
A wedding

THE CONQUER

THE CLIMB

A bulk-sized container of antibacterial wipes
A bad investment
A map

THE CONQUER

THE CLIMB

A vaccination
A slice of cake
A person chasing a departing bus

THE CONQUER

THE CLIMB

A report card with bad grades
A pizza delivery box
A pair of rusty dumbbells

THE CONQUER

THE CLIMB

A binge of a streaming series
A called-off wedding
An approaching car

THE CONQUER

THE CLIMB

A stack of pancakes
A cabin
A portable bar station that is the scene of a dispute

THE CONQUER

THE CLIMB

A hotel party
A fast food meal
A bad case of insomnia

THE CONQUER

THE CLIMB

A cracked cell phone
A rough drive on gravel
A malfunctioning doorbell

THE CONQUER

THE CLIMB

A custody hearing
A common cold
A hectic planning for a holiday weekend

THE CONQUER

THE CLIMB

A VHS tape
A person in a relationship just for its perks
A rip-off item

THE CONQUER

THE CLIMB

A calculator
A person trying to fix a tablet
A cold room

THE CONQUER

THE CLIMB

A bag of hunting gear
A person searching for an assisted living center
A high school corridor

THE CONQUER

An RV for sale
A person who develops health issues from stress
A strand of hair

THE CONQUER

A fruit salad
A person dealing with guilt
A mouse trap

THE CONQUER

A root canal
A person trying to expunge their record
A call to come home as soon as possible

THE CONQUER

THE CLIMB

Tangled hair
A name tag
A pack rat

THE CONQUER

THE CLIMB

An irregular heartbeat
A custodial worker
A green hose

THE CONQUER

THE CLIMB

A pair of siblings with their biggest feud yet
A meerkat
A lock and key

THE CONQUER

THE CLIMB

A person who always speaks too much
A new vehicle
A pocket with a hole

THE CONQUER

THE CLIMB

A wrench
A stand-up comedian
An electrical fire

THE CONQUER

THE CLIMB

A serving of parfait
A diagram
A person with bad coping mechanisms

THE CONQUER

THE CLIMB

A submarine sandwich
An Amber alert
A broken charger

THE CONQUER

THE CLIMB

A parkour competitor
A pumpkin pie slice
A hospital visit

THE CONQUER

THE CLIMB

Two enemies turned pals turned co-conspirators
A phone that goes dead
A lottery ticket

THE CONQUER

A person who misjudges a meal ticket
A skin rash
An art studio

A dealer of narcotics
A social reporter
A piece of formerly unknown information

A person who keeps getting mysteriously sick
A gallon of windshield washer fluid
A loft

THE CLIMB

A sports photographer
A sketchy front office decision
A confiscated weapon

THE CONQUER

THE CLIMB

An Achilles heel: Can be guilt-tripped easily
An object: A skin graft
A conflict: An accusation of embezzlement

THE CONQUER

THE CLIMB

A collectible coin
A trio of pending litigations
An episode of catatonic shock

THE CONQUER

THE CLIMB

A person with a propensity for exaggeration
A boat
A failed scheme

THE CONQUER

THE CLIMB

A strength: High intuition
A conflict: A hearsay discussion
A setting: A skating rink

THE CONQUER

THE CLIMB

An Achilles heel: Ego issues
A conflict: A swimming incident
A setting: A deliberation room

THE CONQUER

THE CLIMB

A sports career cut short in the most unexpected and tragic way...

THE CONQUER

THE CLIMB

A person who gets accused of a misdemeanor...

THE CONQUER

THE CLIMB

A person talking on the phone suddenly goes quiet and starts crying. Because...

THE CONQUER

Challenge: It can't be around a death.

A person who finally gets clean of an addiction only to…

THE CONQUER

THE CLIMB

A teen opens their locker and freezes instantly. They look across the hall to find classmates staring and snickering beecause…

THE CONQUER

THE CLIMB

A person comes home to find everyone crying. Because…

THE CONQUER

THE CLIMB

"As soon as I let you have a bit more freedom, you do THIS!"

THE CONQUER

Challenge: This can't be an upset parent speaking to their child.

THE CLIMB

"I'm beginning to think my life is one big joke that I don't know about."

THE CONQUER

What has made the speaker think this? How will the speaker finally have a new outlook? Document this rise to success.

THE CLIMB

"Get a clue, and get GOING!"

THE CONQUER

Who's saying this? Who are they saying this to? Why are they saying it? How can the person being addressed move forward?

"I like to think I'm getting better. But I can't wait until I'm knowing it and not just thinking it."

THE CONQUER

How will this speaker finally have confidence in themselves? Document this rise to success.

"I'm talking all in. I'm going ALL. IN."

THE CONQUER

All in on what? Will it work in the seemingly confident speaker's favor?

"You know what?...I'm going to try that.

Thanks."

THE CONQUER

Who is the speaker thanking? What did the speaker get as advice? Why is it so impactful? How will the speaker utilize that advice?

THE CLIMB

An Achilles heel: Sore loser
An object: A soda can
A setting: A principal's office

THE CONQUER

THE CONQUER

THE CLIMB

An Achilles heel: A tendency to procastinate
An object: A pair of skates
A setting: A credit counseling center

THE CONQUER

THE CLIMB

An Achilles heel: Social anxiety
An object: A phone app
A conflict: Rising unpaid college debt

THE CONQUER

An Achilles heel: Low self-esteem
An object: A suitcase
A conflict: A rumor

THE CONQUER

THE CLIMB

An Achilles heel: Possessiveness
An object: A rubber band
A setting: A secluded hallway at a party venue

THE CONQUER

THE CLIMB

An Achilles heel: A tendency to instigate
An object: A house deed
A setting: A home rental for a family reunion

THE CONQUER

WRITE TO KEEP ON

keeping on to…

Write to Keep on Flying: Writing Story Prompts for an Out-of-This-World Adventure or Other Children's Novel, Screenplay, or Stageplay

Write to Keep On Crying (TEARS!): Writing Story Prompts for a Laugh-Out-Loud Comedy Novel, Screenplay, or Stageplay

Write to Keep Them Guessing and Excited: Writing Story Prompts for a Provoking Sci-Fi, Fantasy, Thriller/Mystery, or Action Novel, Screenplay, or Stageplay

By Hakeela Buford
on Amazon
&

AF.FORD media.co